Gopal the Infallible

Adapted by Sita Gilbakian

Mandala Publishing Group

From Ancient India come the mystical and enchanting stories of Gopal, the cowherder.

While living the life of a simple village boy, Gopal is actually God himself playing human. His adventures in the forests of Vrindavan bring both joy and amazement to those who hear them.

Endowed with limitless powers and riches, Gopal shows time and time again his greatest strength is his love and affection for his cows, friends and family.

It had been a long morning in the pastures outside Vrindaban Village. Now it was getting late, and all the boys and calves were hungry.

"Here is a nice picnic spot," Gopal said. "After we eat, we can play on the grassy bank of the Yamuna River. The calves can drink the water and graze on the grass."

So the boys let the calves loose and sat down in a big circle to eat their lunch.

The cowherd boys did not see the calves wandering away. The calves wanted to eat the fresh grass of the deep forest. Soon they were entirely out of sight.

Then one of the boys noticed. "Oh no! The calves have disappeared!"

The boys would get in trouble if they lost the calves. "What should we do?" they cried.

Gopal said, "Don't worry. I have almost finished my lunch, so I will look for the calves myself. They cannot be too far away. They have probably just gone into the woods."

Even though Gopal looked like a boy in the cowherding village of Vrindaban, he was the Lord of the Universe. That is why he knew exactly where the calves were. One of the little gods called Brahma had led them away from the river.

Gopal said, "Two can play at being tricksters. I will let Brahma think I am just a little boy."

Gopal searched in the thickets and in the deep forest for the missing calves. He even explored all the nearby mountain caves. He pretended that he could not find the calves.

Brahma, who is in charge of everything in the world, was very powerful. He had so many things to think of, and so many things to create, that he needed four heads!

One day when Brahma thought Gopal was not watching, he led all of Gopal's calves to a secret cave. He waved his four arms and put the calves into a magical sleep.

Then, when Gopal left his friends to search for the missing calves, Brahma made all the cowherd boys go to the same cave. Under Brahma's magical spell, they also fell soundly asleep.

When Gopal could not find his friends, he pretended to be surprised. "I must try to find them."

Once again Gopal looked in the thickets and forest. He explored all the nearby mountain caves and crevices. He searched until it was nearly dark.

But he did not find his friends or calves.

"How can I go back to Vrindaban alone?" Gopal said.

Brahma planned to keep the boys and calves in the cave for only a little while. But he forgot that time passes very slowly in his world. What is one minute for him, is one year on Earth.

"I will show Brahma who is the Master of all Mystics," Gopal said.

He then turned himself into many many boys. Gopal also changed himself into many many calves. Each boy and each calf looked and acted just like one that Brahma had hidden.

The boys played on their flutes, just as they always did. The calves' hooves raised a golden cloud of dust, just as they always did. The boys put the calves into their cowsheds before they went home, just as they always did.

The mothers of Vrindaban Village heard the boys' flutes. They ran out to embrace their sons, just as they always did. Each mother took her son on her lap and hugged him tightly.

Gopal, in the form of each of the cowherd boys, accepted this offering of love from all the mothers.

"It is usually Gopal who holds a special place in my heart," one mother told her son as she gave him a kiss. "Perhaps it is because of all the wonderful things he does. But tonight I feel as if you are stealing that special place in my heart."

The mothers and fathers of Vrindaban Village became more and more fond of the cowherd boys.

Sometimes, for no reason at all, fathers would carry their son in their arms. They did this even though the boy was quite able to walk on his own. Sometimes they stopped their work and played with their sons without even being asked. And sometimes they sang lullabies while their sons lay asleep in bed.

Not one father nor one mother suspected that their own child was asleep in a cave under a magical spell.

During this magical year, the cowherd men led the cows onto a grassy hill. The cowherd boys were grazing the calves on the other side of the hill. As soon as the cows saw the calves on the hill, they ran after them. With milk bags full and tails raised, the cows leapt over the rough paths. They mooed loudly and lovingly licked the calves.

The cowherd men chased after their cows. "Stop those cows!" they called to the boys. But the boys could not stop them.

Gopal's older brother, Balaram, was watching this happen.

"This is not right," he thought. "The cows have new calves to suckle. These calves are too big to still drink from their mothers' milk bags. Has someone cast a magic spell over them to make them act like this?"

Balaram saw the cowherd men chasing the cows. He saw them try to get the cows away from the calves. "Now all the boys are going to be in trouble!" he said. "It is their job to keep the calves separate from their mothers."

But Balaram was wrong.

The cowherd men ran up the hill behind their cows. They were very angry.

But as soon as they reached their sons, they forgot their anger. Instead of chastising them, the men gave the boys big hugs.

"Why are they making such a fuss over the boys?" Balaram wondered. "They just saw each other an hour ago. I think someone has cast a magical spell over Vrindaban Village. I must find Gopal. He will know what is going on. He always knows everything."

Balaram told Gopal, "These are not the same cowherd boys and calves who went grazing last year. Are they some of the gods in disguise? Or is this another one of your wonderful tricks?"

Gopal told Balaram what Brahma had done. He said, "I have made myself look like all of them so that our mothers and fathers are not upset. What would they say if they knew the calves and boys had been kidnapped?"

"But you are the God of all gods," Balaram said. "Why don't you just get the real boys and calves from the cave?"

"I want to trick Brahma," Gopal said.

Brahma said, "I will wake up the calves and boys now." He ordered his magic swan to fly him to Vrindaban Village.

But the boys and calves were already awake. They were playing and laughing with Gopal. Everything was just like before Brahma stole the calves.

Brahma shook his head. "But I put them all to sleep by my mystic spell. Has my powerful magic not worked?"

Brahma forgot how slowly time passes on his planet. He thought only one minute had passed. In his life it had. But on Earth an entire year had come and gone.

Brahma blinked his eyes. When he opened them the cowherd boys each had not two arms, but four! What sort of magic was this? Brahma blinked again. This time each boy grew nearly as big as the sky. Their necklaces were so shiny that they outshone any stars in the sky.

Brahma knew now that these were not cowherd boys. They were his own lord, Vishnu. "How have they become Vishnu?" Brahma wondered. "Who is such a powerful magician to do this?"

Brahma shook his head. "These cowherd boys and calves are not the ones I kidnapped."

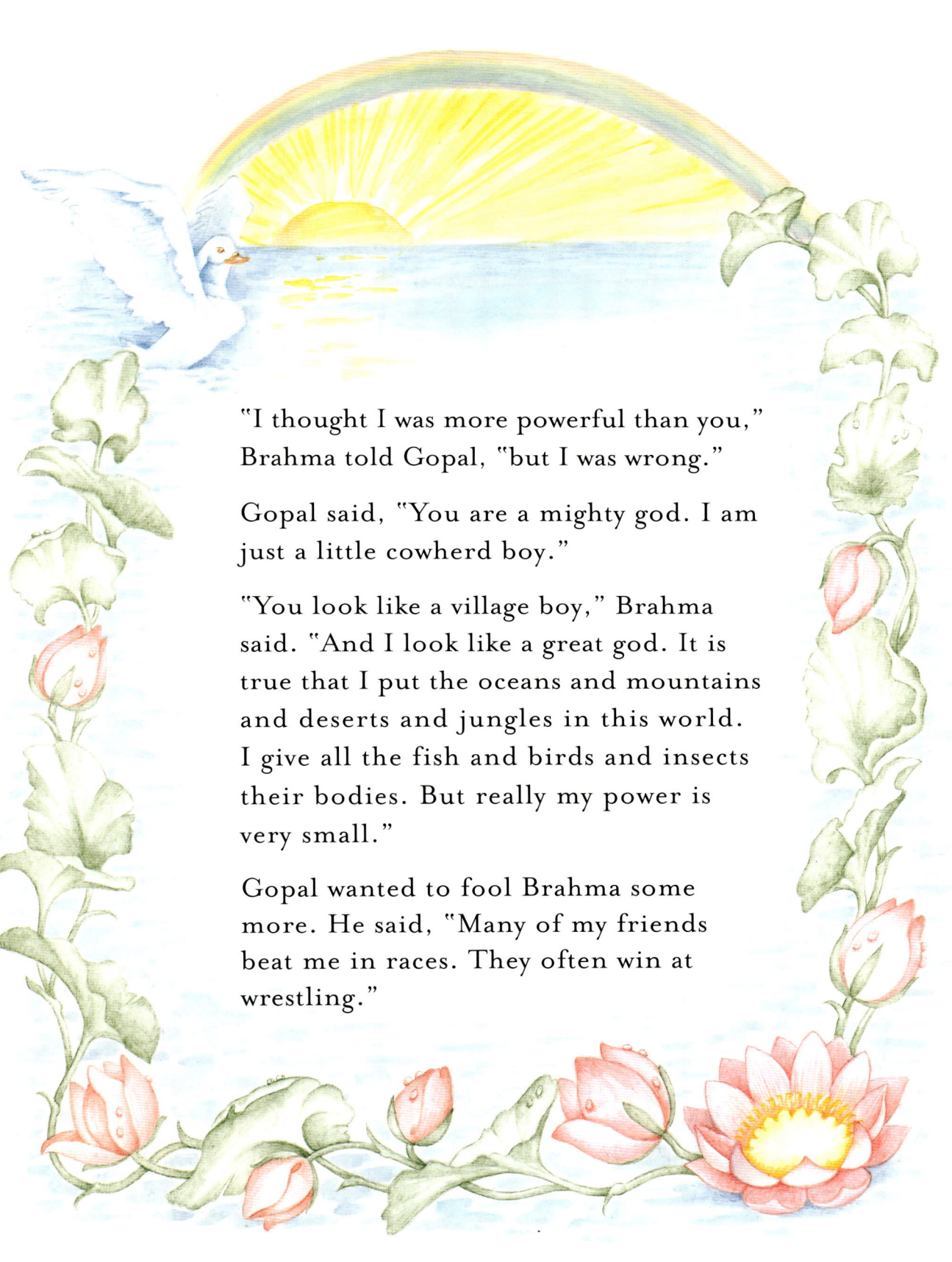

"I thought I was more powerful than you," Brahma told Gopal, "but I was wrong."

Gopal said, "You are a mighty god. I am just a little cowherd boy."

"You look like a village boy," Brahma said. "And I look like a great god. It is true that I put the oceans and mountains and deserts and jungles in this world. I give all the fish and birds and insects their bodies. But really my power is very small."

Gopal wanted to fool Brahma some more. He said, "Many of my friends beat me in races. They often win at wrestling."

Gopal told Brahma, "Each day I go to the pasturing grounds with my friends. Today I have lost my friends and calves. If you know where they might be, please tell me."

"You have not lost your friends," Brahma said. "I tried to steal them from you. But I could not trick you. You are the Supreme Lord. Everything comes from you. You have shown me that you can become everything. But still you stay different from everything. Please forgive me for being so foolish."

Brahma returned to his own planet. He would never again try to test Gopal's mystic powers.

Gopal went to the cave where Brahma had hidden the boys and calves. They were all still deep asleep in a trance. Gopal used his divine powers to bring them back to the bank of the River Yamuna.

When the boys woke up they said, "Gopal has returned so quickly. Were the calves far away?"

"We have not even finished our lunch yet," one boy said.

Gopal smiled and sat down to eat lunch. He did not tell them just how long he had been gone.

This exciting new line of beautifully illustrated children's books presents a charming and endearing narrative of the pastimes of Gopal.

Miraculous Gopal

When the village of Vrindavan is inundated with torrential rains sent by the furious King of Heaven, Indra, Gopal displays his divinity by lifting Govardhan Hill and saving the cows and all of the inhabitants of Vrindavan. Indra is humbled and offers prayers to Gopal accepting him as the Supreme Person.

$14.95 hardbound, 48 pages
Item 1211

The Gift of Gopal

In this third part of the Gopal trilology, Gopal has grown up and is Krishna, ruler of Dvarka. One of Gopal's childhood friends is encouraged by his wife to visit Krishna and ask him to alleviate their poverty. Upon seeing Krishna, this friend is overwhelmed with joy and is completely content, forgetting his request. However, Krishna manages to answer his friends forgotten questions and desires.

$14.95 hardbound, 48 pages
Item1213

Order now by calling 800 688 2218
Have your Visa or Master Casrd ready
Alternatively, send a check or money order to:
Mandala Publishing Group
103 Thomason Lane   Eugene, OR 97404

To our young Readers
who are always eager
to hear the pastimes of
our friend Gopal.

Mandala Publishing Group
47 Beach Road
05-06, Kheng Chui Bldg.
Singapore, 189683
65 339 6965 phone
65 339 6670 fax

103 Thomason Lane
Eugene, OR 97404 U.S.A.
541 688 2258 phone
541 461 3478 fax

mandala@cyberis.net
www.mandala.org

Printed in Hong Kong through Palace Press International

ISBN 1-886069-17-4
© Mandala Publishing Group 1998
All rights reserved